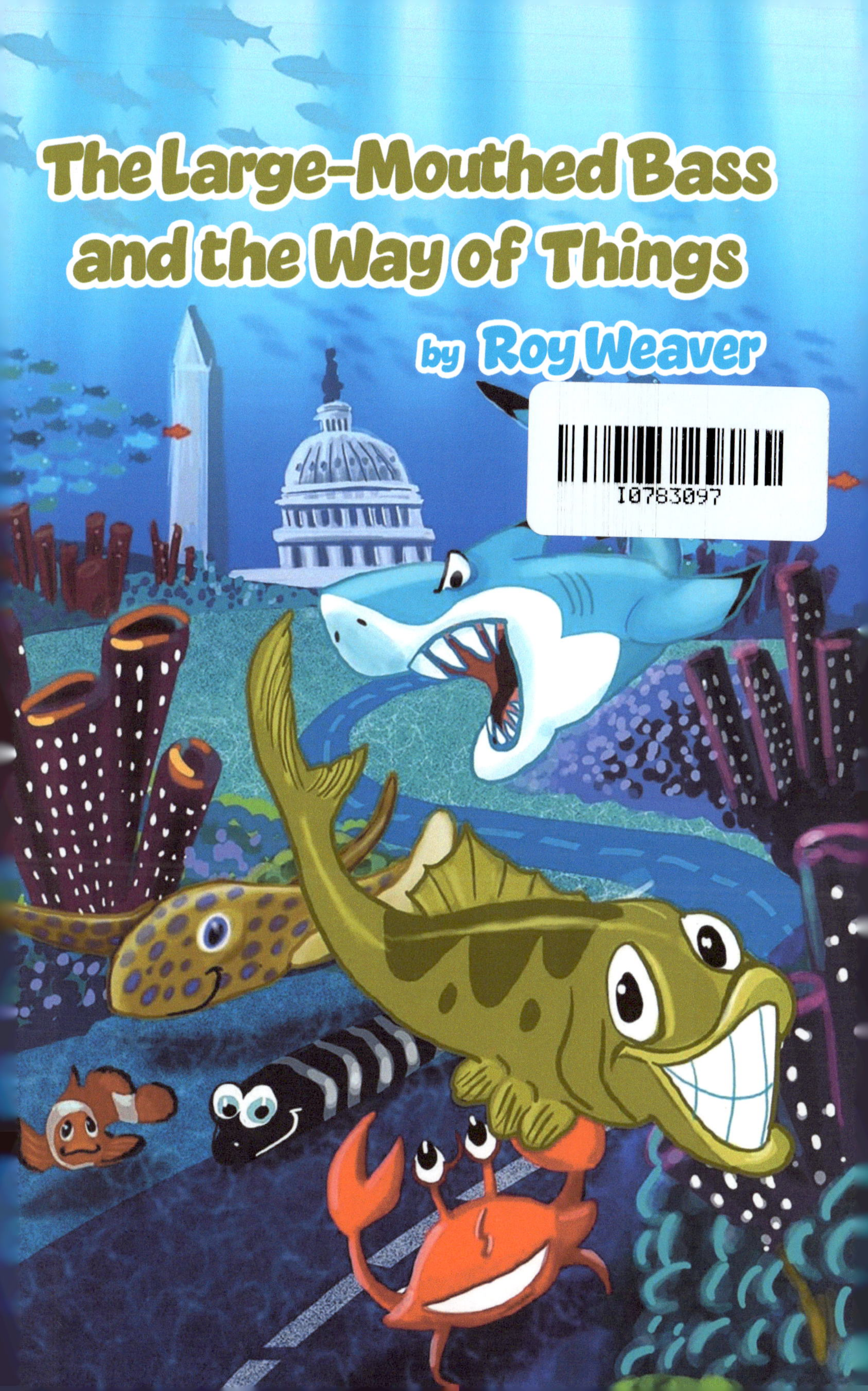

The Large-Mouthed Bass
and the Way of Things
by Roy Weaver
I0783097

long time ago, when the earth was covered with water, there were many different species of fish, swimming, playing, and working in the vast oceans. They could be seen darting and dashing through the swift currents and sparkling beams of sunlight with not a care but their freedom to be happy and dream of a wonderful "Way of Things". There were also other species of crawly creatures in many strange and wonderful shapes, sizes, colors and characters that shared the seemingly endless underwater world. The ocean world was an endless landscape with intricate patterns of rocky nooks, deep crevasses, lush green underwater forests, and vast desolate open spaces. Scattered across the ocean were occasional mountain ranges rising to the ocean surface with an explosion of activity in and around the multi-colored oasis at the top. Each oasis was like an ocean city built on top of older cities over long periods of time. Ocean cities are known as reefs where the Hard-Working Fish flourished and multiplied. Within each species of fish, and other forms of plants and creatures, there were those that produced the children of the next generation and those that nurtured and instructed each new generation in the Way of Things. Each species maintained this delicate life balance to ensure survival and harmony throughout the ocean. This was the Way of Things.

As time passed, some of the larger, more powerful fish began to believe they were superior in strength and intellect to the other species. They had steely eyes and rows of sharp gnashing teeth. They also believed they were the elite social class of their own species and especially all the other smaller and weaker fish in the ocean. This particularly brazen bunch of bullies was known as Politi-Sharks. Politi-Sharks were the worst of the shark species. The superior elitist Politi-Sharks were mean, scary-looking ominous creatures that spent their time scheming and planning to take over control of the reef societies. Politi-Sharks were deceitful liars. Their only weakness was their incredibly thin skin.

TAXES
MENU

Politi-Sharks took advantage of the other fish by making promises to ensure their safety and security, only to break those promises and often leave the Hard-Working Fish to fend for themselves. Politi-Sharks were devious bullies who could prevent any lesser creature from pursuing a happy and prosperous life by denying them the liberties they always believed were guaranteed. Using fearmongering and the threat of losing their liberties, Politi-Sharks convinced the other fish that there should be laws and punishment established to regulate behavior across the reef societies. The Politi-Sharks created a process whereby the Hard-Working Fish could get together and vote to choose which species would make the laws. The laws were the rule of the land that all fish would live by and thus bring order to the reefs. The voting process was deceiving to the Hard-Working Fish since the voter choice was always a Politi-Shark. Since the Politi-Sharks made the laws, they convinced the fish that Politi-Sharks should choose the enforcers of the laws who would protect the fish from the dangers of the ocean. The Politi-Sharks' feelings of superiority were not based on just their imposing, scary physical characteristics, it was also because the Politi-Sharks had inflated egos about their own purpose in the ocean as they believed they were better than all the other fish. Politi-Sharks felt that they should "Reign in

Dominion" like kings over all the other species. Their "better than everyone else" attitude upset the balance and harmony throughout the ocean world. In some cases, Politi-Sharks would create armies among the other fish species, including other species of sharks. The fish armies were ordered to attack and conquer neighboring reefs. The result would be Politi-Sharks allowing other sharks to force the conquered fish into slavery to serve the sharks by claiming and declaring dominion over them. Thus, enforcing the social class system among the ocean creatures became the new Way of Things.

The fish that were weaker, less knowledgeable, and unable to defend themselves, were conquered, manipulated, enslaved, and abused for many centuries. The Hard-Working Fish became appalled by the mere idea of enslaving other fish. They could imagine that they would eventually be conquered and enslaved under such deplorable circumstances. Every once in a while, a determined group of the more courageous Hard-Working Fish would long for the freedom they remembered from the old Way of Things. They would secretly plan, prepare, and attempt to incite a revolution against the Politi-Sharks. Sometimes they would succeed with help from fish of other reefs and establish their own society with their own rules and a form of organized leadership. They called their free but organized society a government of the fish, by the fish, for the fish.

Eventually the Politi-Sharks would infiltrate, spy on, attack, and conquer these self-governing Hard-Working Fish colonies. Having the greater more overpowering force allowed the Politi-Sharks to once again reign in dominion over their empire. The Politi-Sharks often used other fish to secretly spy for them and infiltrate the Hard-Working Fish government. The spy fish were offered special favors and feelings of superiority by making them exempt from the laws and punishment Politi-Sharks imposed on the rest of the reef societies. The Politi-Sharks would have their infil-traitors organize groups of Hard-Working Fish and convince them that life would be better if Politi-Sharks assigned more intelligent helpers to represent the Hard-Working Fish in negotiating for benefits and liberties with the Politi-Sharks. The helper fish were very much like sharks, but they were a different species known as the Barracuda. Acting as a ruthless ally of the

Politi-Sharks, Barracudas were encouraged by the Politi-Sharks to establish an organized governing network of their own, called the Inter-Ocean Worker-Fish Organization. It was the first time that an acronym was used to identify such an organization. The acronym was officially called the IWO. The Politi-Sharks and Barracudas in charge of the IWO shared the benefits and authority of reigning in dominion over the Hard-Working Fish. The Politi-Sharks were the ruling class who made the oppressive controlling laws, and the Barracuda would prevent the Hard-Working Fish from rising up on their own to challenge the Politi-Sharks' dominion over them. The ruling class Politi-Fish always had plenty of the finest food and never wanted for anything but greater dominion over other fish. They could move about the ocean doing and saying anything to instill fear in the hearts and minds of every other ocean creature. Politi-Sharks had no regard or respect for the laws they made, and the Barracuda were exempt from the laws since they were the enforcers of the laws. This became the new Way of Things.

Even though some fish worked extremely hard and were able to become quite successful, the sharks kept tight control over life and resources in the ocean. The fish grew complacent and became preoccupied with trivial things like playing games and other entertainment activities. Some of the games included challenges between teams from different reefs upon which the Hard-Working Fish could gamble and bet their precious belongings, more often losing than winning. It became another way for the Barracudas to manipulate and control the Hard-Working Fish. The Politi-Sharks watched intently from their lofty world. Politi-Sharks found it to be a useful method of manipulation and entertainment by pitting certain species, and even individual fish, against each other to ensure there would be no more thoughts of a united revolt against the Politi-Sharks.

Politi-Sharks confidently assured themselves that everything they did to maintain dominion relied on what sharks called, the stupidity of the average ocean creature. Politi-Sharks had total control to dictate the most ridiculous laws, rules, and regulations to make all the Hard-Working Fish act outside their natural behavior. Chaos amongst the fish was a good thing. It would keep the fish from realizing how they were being manipulated by the Politi-Sharks in their quest for absolute dominion. This was the Way of Things.

As many beautiful flourishing reefs began to slowly deteriorate into a less colorful and more depressing state of things, the fish had to work harder to find food and provide security for their families. The Politi-Sharks had taken control of all the social institutions like family, education, and personal beliefs. Politi-Sharks controlled all aspects of education so only what they wanted the young fish to believe was taught in the fish schools. The Politi-Sharks had control of family values whereby they discouraged independent ways of teaching children if it was not the way young fish were being taught in the schools. The Hard-Working Fish tried to hold on to their social and moral beliefs, but their basic individual identity was stolen from them and replaced by one which was acceptable to the collective Politi-Shark and Barracuda run society.

Politi-Sharks would deny access to resources or take away the once-guaranteed freedoms and liberties from the Hard-Working Fish to keep them in a constant state of struggle.

Some of the more prominent and successful worker fish from the entertainment industries would isolate themselves at a reef where they had the freedom to prosper, express their beliefs, and protect themselves from the common fish class laws and rules to enjoy the freedom and liberties that were denied elsewhere. Other more prosperous fish, like those in the construction industry that built the reefs, enjoyed more freedoms and prosperity than the regular working fish. These fish were necessary for society but often demonized by the Politi-Sharks because they actually had a useful skill. Many of the successful and prosperous fish gave up their ownership rights in order to gain favor from the Politi-Sharks. In return, they shared their prosperous gains with Politi-Sharks. Only the successful fish that had something to offer to the lifestyle of the Politi-Sharks were ever allowed to prosper. The hard working, middle class fish ultimately became very weary of the constant oppression by the Politi-Sharks. At first, the Hard-Working Fish were glad and proud to take on the responsibility of helping those less fortunate. They felt especially generous when giving to those who were victims of circumstances that made life more challenging. The Politi-Sharks ultimately convinced more fish that they were victims of life's challenges and deserved a greater share from Hard-Working Fish to support them all as one large collective. Life became exceedingly difficult for the Hard-Working Fish who were made to feel guilty and were often punished for not giving enough to support all the demands of each new generation. The younger fish were taught in the schools that the liberties and freedom they did get came from the Politi-Sharks and all such gifts were never guaranteed in life and must be shared with fish from other reefs. Even greater frustration began spreading across all the reefs in the ocean as the resources diminished. Hard-Working Fish tried many times in desperate vain to have some sort of compassionate representation among the Politi-Sharks for the fish that gave everything to the fish that got everything. They would vote again and again to send representatives to Politi-Shark City, where the Politi-Shark central government was located, only to find out they sent a Barracuda, or another species of shark in Hard-Working Fish disguise that would become a Politi-Shark. This became the Way of Things.

One day, as if by destiny, a beam of sunlight penetrated the surface of the ocean and glistened off the golden head of a very prosperous and successful fish who had risen to prominent prosperity. This particular fish had become popular because of his association with some of the Politi-Fish and his seemingly agreeable nature in the Politi-Shark world. He was known for his generosity to those less fortunate and played in the entertainment arena to amass charitable contributions for many giving organizations.

It was a time when even the most prosperous of Hard-Working Fish realized that enough was enough from the Politi-Sharks' oppressing, abusing, manipulating, and reign of dominion over life in the ocean. Of all the fish, in all the ocean, this flamboyant celebrity fish was known as a Large-Mouthed Bass. The Large-Mouthed Bass was not considered a political government type species and not expected to be accepted by Politi-Sharks in their world. He was, after all, a Large-Mouthed Bass. He did not care what the consequences might be for what he would say about Politi-Sharks, or anyone else for that matter. He was not necessarily trusted by other fish species to be a leader in Politi-Shark City. The Hard-Working Fish had been sending other fish of every species to represent them in Politi-Shark City for many years. The supposedly trustworthy representatives would make many promises, more than the Hard-Working Fish could remember, and they kept only one. They promised to take away the fishes' rights to freedom and liberty, and they took them. The Large-Mouthed Bass decided to use all his own personal resources, his bold character, brash words, and power of persuasion to enter the contest for being selected by vote to represent all the hard-working, oppressed, and struggling fish in Politi-Shark City. This angered the Politi-Sharks immensely. They challenged the

Large-Mouthed Bass with more than a dozen Politi-Sharks and Barracudas in what was called an election. Even the Barracudas were very confident that any one of them could defeat the Large-Mouthed Bass. They could put a stop to his ridiculous attempt to even be considered as Leader-in-Chief of the fish in Politi-Shark City. The Large-Mouthed Bass was once just a big fish on a small reef and was not familiar with the ways of Politi-Sharks. However, With the growing enthusiasm and support of many multitudes of fish and ocean creatures, the Large-Mouthed Bass grew in popularity as the greatest Hard-Working Fish in the ocean. His celebrity was well known. He became famous to the Hard-Working Fish and Infamous to the Politi-Sharks who really hated the Large-Mouthed Bass. Many of the Hard-Working Fish were convinced it was impossible for the Large-Mouthed Bass to compete with even one Politi-Shark.

Surprisingly, the Large-Mouthed Bass was able to eventually defeat the crooked Politi-Sharks and their corrupt, disingenuous, super evil supporters at their own game of thrones. The not so hard working fish were so shocked with his victory that many of them developed mental illness over the whole situation. Sadly, many of the not so hard working fish had been convincingly indoctrinated in fish schools by the previous reigning Politi-Shark's academic elitist friends. They had no interest or choice but to remain loyal to the social and political correctness imposed upon them by the previous Way of Things. The entire social and political correctness generation was never taught the old Way of Things. They could not understand how things could be better than the life of personal and social compromise to which they had become accustomed.

PRESS

The misinformed minions of the Politi-Sharks had become so used to their Way of Things that all they could do was hate the Large-Mouthed Bass for trying to bring back the freedoms and liberties of governing themselves, as was once taught in the fish schools. The academic elitist fish even created a movement called the Anti-Fish who would destroy the prosperity of their own reefs to discourage the Hard-Working Fish from supporting the Large-Mouthed Bass.

Hard-Working Fish believed it would be their last chance to stop the relentless drive of the Politi-Sharks from establishing absolute dominion over their united reefs, and eventually, all the reefs of the ocean. Throughout his quest to become leader of the Hard-Working Fish, the Large-Mouthed Bass had to contend with the most fearsome and egregious of all the species of sharks. The Great White Politi-Shark had ocean-wide resources and connections to the most sinister of ocean creatures, the Killer Politi-Whales. Killer Polit-Whales resources, connections and ocean influence were limitless. Politi-Sharks, and many of the ocean's fish, believed the Large-Mouthed Bass certainly and positively could not be accepted in Politi-Shark City, especially as their leader.

The fancy looking, constantly chatting fish, responsible for broadcasting the news and truth across the reefs, and even the entire ocean, were known as Media Parrot Fish. Media Parrot Fish were watched closely by Polit-Sharks and expected, but never trusted to tell all Hard-Working Fish the truth about the Way of Things. Even after the Large-Mouthed

Bass defeated the Great White Politi-Shark in the voter election, the Media Parrot Fish continuously denounced the Large-Mouthed Bass. Media Parrot Fish spent all their time and effort attempting to destroy, denigrate, and assassinate Large-Mouthed Bass' personal and professional character. The Way of Things became very divisive and created two distinct opposing sides to every single question or issue that existed in the ocean. The Politi-Sharks in Politi-Shark City had no intention of ever giving up their lavish lifestyle with all the perks, parties, and benefits of reigning in dominion over the reefs and all the Hard-Working Fish. Having a Large-Mouthed Bass in their midst would expose their sinister ways and disrupt the entire Way of Things.

The Politi-Sharks in Politi-Shark City could get away with saying or doing anything to ensure they would continue to reign in dominion over the ocean. The Media Parrot Fish would take their cue from the Politi-Sharks and repeat their hateful and disingenuously fake message over and over again until it became truthful fact. Because so many of the fish had been indoctrinated in the Shark Way of Things, the Great White Politi-Sharks used the benefit of manipulating their thoughts through the Media Parrot Fish to the fullest advantage. The Large-Mouthed Bass would also try to say whatever he wanted in the Parrot Fish Media, but the Politi-Sharks and Media Parrot Fish would often use his own words against him. Politi-Sharks understood how susceptible the Large-Mouthed Bass would be to going after tried and true Politi-Shark bait. The Great Whites were relentless in generating hatred toward the Large-Mouthed Bass. More and more angry fish became even more angry and hateful toward each other without even knowing why. One or two of the more insightful Media Parrot Fish started to reveal how the Great White Politi-Sharks had been less than honest in dealing with Hard-Working Fish, including other Politi-Sharks. In fact, it was being revealed that many of the Politi-Sharks and Barracuda had been disingenuous in their reign of dominion over the reefs for centuries. More and more frustrated Hard-Working Fish began to support the Large-Mouthed Bass. But the Large-Mouthed Bass was still out of his league and had to constantly watch his tail. Several superior and elite thinking Oceanist Killer Whales started to help the Great White Politi-Sharks and refused to support the Large-Mouthed Bass. Especially those in charge of the Media Parrot Fish. The Great White Politi-Sharks even threatened to, but could not consider assassinating the Large-Mouthed Bass. The assassination tactic had been done too often in the past when any ocean creature, including a Politi-Shark or Barracuda, disrupted the Way of Things in Politi-Shark City. Because of the hatred toward the Large-Mouthed Bass, it would be way too obvious to the Hard-Working Fish that the Great White Politi-Sharks were as extremely corrupt and criminally crooked as way in the past. The evil Great White Politi-Sharks intimidated, manipulated, and directed the Barracudas and the Media Parrot Fish. Barracudas were ordered to attack and try to take bites from the tail of the Large-Mouthed Bass until he could no longer swim with the fishes. The Great White Politi-Sharks hoped they could make the Large-Mouthed Bass give up and Politi-Shark City would return to their Way of Things.

The Large-Mouthed Bass strongly believed that there will never be another chance for the Hard-Working Fish to once again raise their own children, be secure in their reefs and homes, be able to do and speak without oppression or repression, and return to the Way of Things before sharks reigned in dominion. The Politi-Sharks believed that if they stop the Large-Mouthed Bass, and prepare for any such free-spirited creature to ever see the light of the surface again, life in the ocean will return to the Politi-Shark Correct Way of Things. And, they shall reign in dominion for all time. The next generations of Politi-Sharks would have the freedom to reimagine the ocean world as some kind of perfect utopian social order. Politi-Sharks will reign in dominion while all the Hard-Working Fish follow the rules and continue to be preoccupied with their selfish lives until the end of things.

The Large-Mouthed Bass and the Way of Things will one day end with a new beginning, as all things do in the world. Will the Large-Mouthed Bass be able to continue defeating the Great White Politi-Sharks, withstand the relentless attacks from the Media Parrot Fish, and stand up to the Oceanist, Killer Politi-Whales? Can the Large-Mouthed Bass stand on his own or will a new freedom-loving independent generation rise to the surface to protect and defend the Hard-Working Fish? Will all the Hard-Working Fish of the ocean ever be able to return to the Way of Things that was once the law of the creator and the law of nature, before the laws of Politi-Sharks gave them the power to reign in dominion?

Someday the waters will recede to reveal the great rocky reefs that once rose from the icy depths to the sunny surface of the vast ocean. The lofty and majestic mountains will rise to the heavens as if reigning in dominion over the world. The flourishing forests, the glorious green and golden plains, and the vast oceans, will present new species of creatures that will inhabit the world. One such creature will be known as humans. Some humans will strive to reign in dominion over all other Hard-Working Humans. Humans will one day establish societies with organized governments and live according to their own laws and order. Will the human Way of Things be based on the laws of their creator, the laws of nature, or the laws of humans? Will some Politi-Humans have such a superior opinion of themselves that they will defy both the laws of their creator and the laws of nature to create the laws of humans for the purpose of reigning in dominion over other humans?

Perhaps the purpose for every creature, from the greatest to the least in size and significance in all the oceans and across all the land, is to reflect some behavior or characteristic of the greatest and most susceptible creature to the lust for dominion over all creatures, including their own.

Global domination, and the quest for dominion by humans over other humans, has caused some of the most devastating consequences to both humans and nature. Some of the most beautiful and impressive creatures of the land and oceans have been forced into a life-and-death struggle for survival. Sadly, many species will never be seen again, or will become extremely rare, or even extinct. What creatures of the oceans, land, and skies will be left in this world to reflect our character and soul back to ourselves? Will they swim in the ocean, soar in the skies, or crawl in and out of the darkest dingy slimy swamps? Will they survive by feeding on the death and destruction caused by the relentless and evil quest by those that are driven to reign in dominion? What will become the "Way of Things"?